GETS HIS WISH

Original script by Ken Scarborough

Adapted by Eric Suben

Illustrated by Chris Nowell, William Presing, Jeff Nodelman

Original characters for "The Funnies" developed by Jim Jinkins and Joe Aaron

A GOLDEN BOOK • NEW YORK

Golden Books Publishing Company, Inc., New York, New York, 10106

 Library of Congress Catalog Card Number: 98-85741 ISBN: 0-307-13140-8 R MM

Dear Journal,

It's me—Doug.

As usual, this morning I still had some leftover homework. There's always a ton of homework to do for Ms. Kristal's class because she really tries to get us into reading . . .

. . . books like DR. JEKYLL AND MR. HYDE, . . .
MOBY DICK, . . .

and PETER PAN. (We're still trying
to figure out how she did that flying thing.)

But I don't complain about it anymore. Now I just do the homework and run to class. See, a few weeks ago I learned my lesson. We were in Ms. Kristal's class studying this book called ANIMAL FARM, when the principal's son Willy came in late. Then Willy didn't know the answer to a really easy question, so Ms. Kristal kept him after class.

That's when all the trouble started.

That afternoon Skeeter and I were in the library trying to find a poem to memorize for Ms. Kristal's class.

"Here's one," Skeeter said. "It's called 'Poetry Is a Destructive Force.'"

"Cool!" I said, until I saw how many lines it had. "Why can't we have a teacher who gives less homework?"

Well, I got my wish. At the next class, Ms. Kristal was gone. Principal White was at her desk.

"I've decided to take this class into my own hands," he said.

I guess Principal White didn't like Ms. Kristal getting Willy into trouble.

Things changed in a hurry. Instead of ANIMAL FARM, Principal White gave us a new assignment.

"I want everyone to get the new Super Stretcho Elasto Man comic book and read it over before tomorrow," he said.

Most of us liked our new assignment. But Skeeter was really beginning to miss Ms. Kristal.

The next day Skeeter tried to start a petition to get Ms. Kristal back, but nobody wanted to sign.

"Principal White is so easy," said Connie.

"Yeah, why would you want Ms. Kristal back?" asked Beebe. "She was hard."

Finally, even though I had enjoyed not having homework, I signed the petition because Skeeter was my friend. But I was the only one who signed.

Patti tried to cheer Skeeter up.

"Principal White is too busy to teach all the time," she said. "He'll probably get someone to replace him before you know it!"

Patti didn't know how right she was. The very next day Principal White was called out of class. But before he left the room, he asked Willy to take over.

Skeeter couldn't stand it. "Bring back Ms. Kristal!" he called out.

Patti tried to cheer Skeeter up.

"Principal White is too busy to teach all the time," she said. "He'll probably get someone to replace him before you know it!"

Patti didn't know how right she was. The very next day Principal White was called out of class. But before he left the room, he asked Willy to take over.

Skeeter couldn't stand it. "Bring back Ms. Kristal!" he called out.

"You want homework again?" Willy shouted back. "Why should we do more work? Let's give the teachers homework!"

The kids all cheered. Of course, I didn't buy any of it.

(Well, maybe I bought it a little bit.)

Since Principal White never came back to class, Willy was our teacher all the time. Homework was a breeze. Usually we had to read a Super Stretcho Elasto Man comic book.

Oh, and we had tests, too—like how many Ring Dilly Dings we could eat. Skeeter was sure that our brains were shrinking from inactivity.

I knew Skeeter was right. But I had to admit, those Ring Dilly Dings were tasty.

One night I went to the store for Mom. I was having a little trouble with the groceries when I heard a familiar voice. "Doug?" it said.

"Ms. Kristal!" I cried. "Everybody misses you. Especially Skeeter."

"Well, I'm afraid that I wasn't getting through too well," Ms. Kristal said with a sigh.

Walking home, I felt pretty awful.

"She was getting through," I told myself. "Skeeter's right. She was a good teacher, even if she did make us learn long poems."

I guess I'd forgotten how much I liked Ms. Kristal.

Willy heard about my meeting with Ms. Kristal.

"It looks like you're plotting against me," he said. "And whoever is against me is gonna get it."

"He can talk to anybody he likes," said Skeeter. "It's a free country!"

"You wish!" Willy told Skeeter. "You're dispended from school."

"*Dispended*?!?!" Skeeter couldn't believe it! "There isn't even such a word as *dispended*!"

Skeeter wasn't the only one who was unhappy. With report cards coming out, Willy had all of us by the throat. He thought up all kinds of tests.

Beebe had to feed him pie.

Connie had to clean his locker.

He even made us say a pledge: "I pledge allegiance to Willy White, whose dad is principal, and he's all-powerful. . . ."

That was the last straw. All the kids got together at Swirly's. "Somebody has to stop Willy," Connie said.

"Even if it means homework again?" I asked.

"Anything," Beebe replied. "Just as long as I don't have to say that dopey pledge."

Suddenly it hit me. "I know how we can prove to everyone that Ms. Kristal is a great teacher!"

First I asked Mayor Tippy to bring up Ms. Kristal's case at the school board meeting. Then I had to wait for just the right moment. . . .

Principal White couldn't wait to speak at the meeting. "My son Willy didn't learn anything!" he told the school board.

"Duh, I never learned a single thing," Willy added.

Then I stood up. "I just want to ask Willy a question," I said.

"I just want to ask Willy if he remembers when Ms. Kristal read us that book about that sea captain named Moby Dick," I said.

Willy answered right back. "Why don't you get it right?" he shouted. "The *whale* is Moby Dick, doof. The guy's name is Captain Ahab."

I tried the same trick again. "Willy, remember how Dr. Jekyll fought that monster, Mr. Hyde?"

"You got it all wrong, Doug!" Willy answered. "They were the same guy. It's like an allegory about the good and evil that live in all of us."

"Gee, Willy," said Principal White, "did Ms. kristal really teach you to be so smart?"

We got Ms. Kristal back. And before we knew it, life in her class was back to normal. We started reading FRANKENSTEIN, and Ms. Kristal really got into it.

Some things were different, though. Willy ended up tutoring the whole gang. And Mayor Tippy asked Ms. Kristal to add a new student to her class—Principal White!

Well, that taught me an important lesson. I guess sometimes things that come easily aren't necessarily good for you. Next time, I'm going to be careful what I wish for!